This Walker book belongs to:

_____

_____

_____

To Louise

First published 2010 by Walker Books Ltd, 87 Vauxhall Walk, London SE11 5HJ

This edition published 2011

2 4 6 8 10 9 7 5 3 1

© 2010 Michael Foreman

The right of Michael Foreman to be identified as author/illustrator of this work has been asserted by him in accordance with the Copyright, Designs and Patents Act 1988

This book has been typeset in ITC Bookman

Printed in China

British Library Cataloguing in Publication Data:

a catalogue record for this book is available from the British Library

ISBN 978-1-4063-2995-7

www.walker.co.uk

WHY the ANIMALS CAME to TOWN

Michael Foreman

WALKER BOOKS
AND SUBSIDIARIES
LONDON · BOSTON · SYDNEY · AUCKLAND

I was woken by the strangest sound,

Quiet at first, but getting louder...

The tramp, tramp, tramp of marching feet,

Louder and louder, down our street!

I peeped round the curtain

And in the evening light

Saw coming round the corner

The most amazing sight.

Every kind of animal

From all around the world –

All coming down our street!

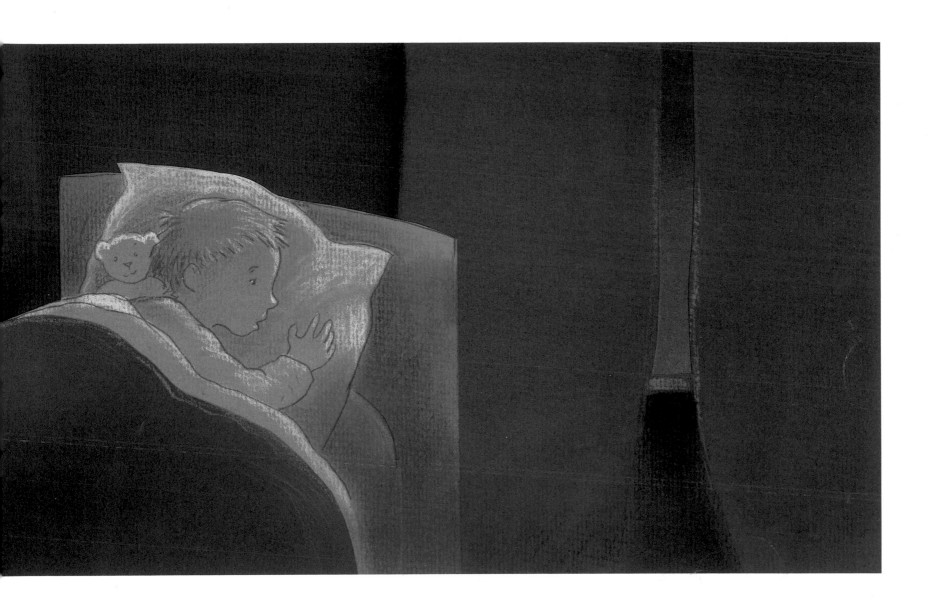

From the north came polar bears

And reindeer, two by two.

From way out west came grizzly bears

And moose and caribou.

From the south came penguins and kangaroos

With pandas from the east.

Out of Africa
came elephants
And a herd
of wildebeest.

Anteaters, apes
    and antelope,
Armadillos and koalas.
Baboons and bison,
    beavers, bats,
Ostriches and meerkats.
Hippos, rhinos,
    chimpanzees,
Monkeys, moose
    and wallabies,
Leopards, lizards,
    lions and llamas –

All coming down our street!

Around the world
    the animals came,
And danced and pranced –
All down our street!

And as they danced
They sang this song,
"Wakey-wakey,
    everyone!
You've been asleep
    for far too long.
Our world is burning,
    melting, sinking.
Everywhere there's
    rubbish stinking.

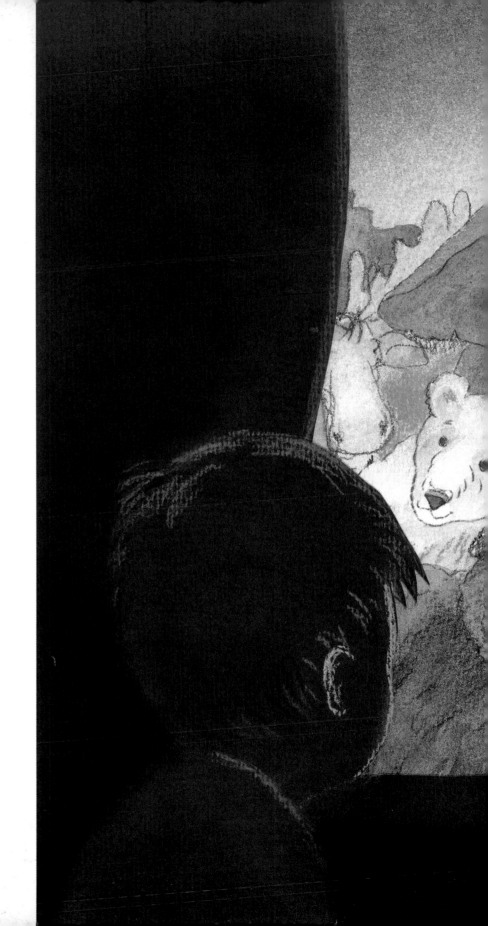

There are dusty deserts

where nothing grows.

And rising seas,

and melting snows.

Smoke fills the sky and hides the sun.

We think it's time something was done."

Then an elephant
scooped me from
my room
And in the cool light
of the moon
The animals and I
danced all night long
Under the starry sky.

Around the town
and through
the park,
Dancing, dancing
in the dark.
By the river,
in the square,
Wonderful animals
everywhere.

As the sun came up
    they took me home
And waved goodbye
    and then were gone.

Our street was empty
    in the dawn.

I saw them there! I really did!

    I really, really, really did!

I hope you saw them too.

And I hope you felt the same as me,

    How empty all the world would be

Without the animals roaming free.

We can help to spread the word,

    It's time the animals' song was heard.

Let's spread their message, you and me.

    That's why the animals came, you see.

Other titles by Michael Foreman

ISBN 978-1-4063-0533-3

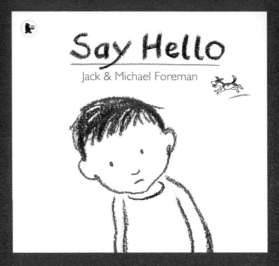

ISBN 978-1-4063-1359-8

ISBN 978-1-4063-2588-1

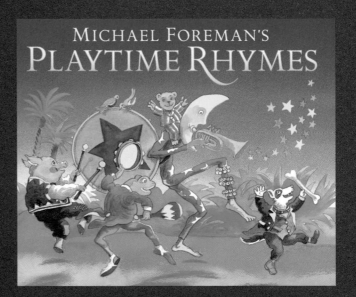

ISBN 978-1-84428-495-5

Available in all good bookstores • www.walker.co.uk